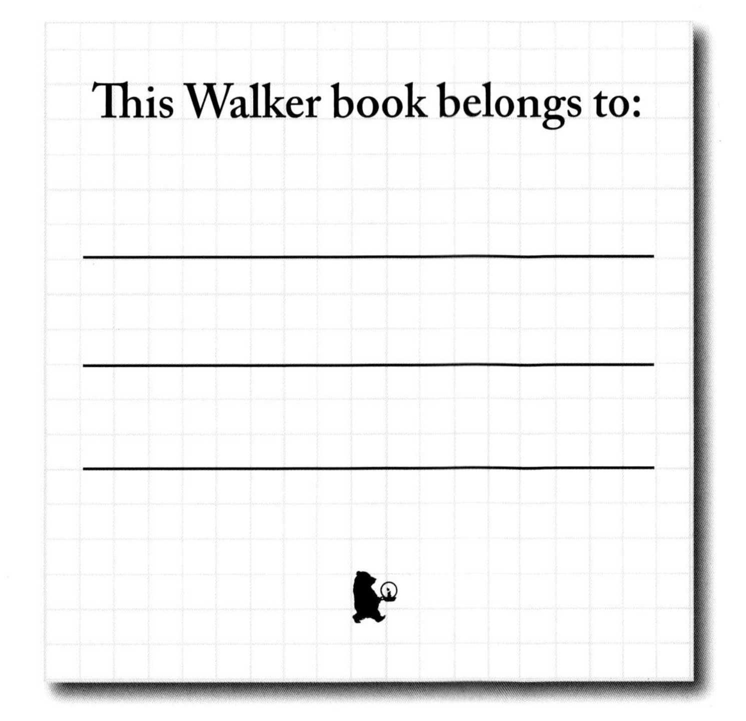
This Walker book belongs to:

First published in the UK in 2015 by Walker Books Ltd
87 Vauxhall Walk, London SE11 5HJ

This edition published 2016

2 4 6 8 10 9 7 5 3 1

This book has been typeset in Futura

Printed in China

British Library Cataloguing in Publication Data:
a catalogue record for this book is available from the British Library

ISBN 978-1-4063-6557-3

www.walker.co.uk

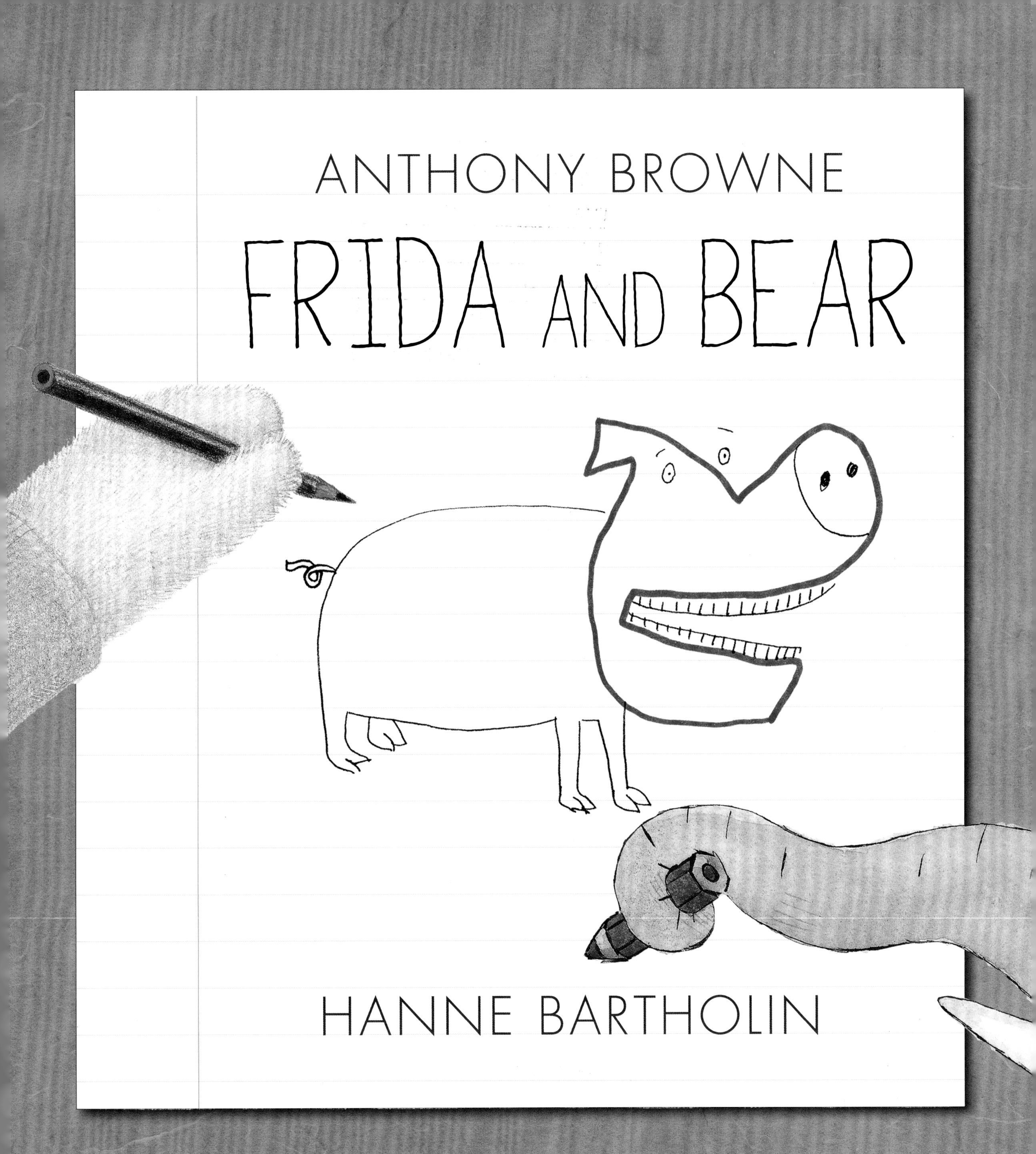
ANTHONY BROWNE
FRIDA AND BEAR
HANNE BARTHOLIN

Frida loved to draw.

And so did Bear.
But one day Bear couldn't think of anything to draw.
"What can I draw, Frida?" he said.

Frida drew a shape,
and gave it to Bear.

"Try and turn this shape into something, Bear,"
said Frida.

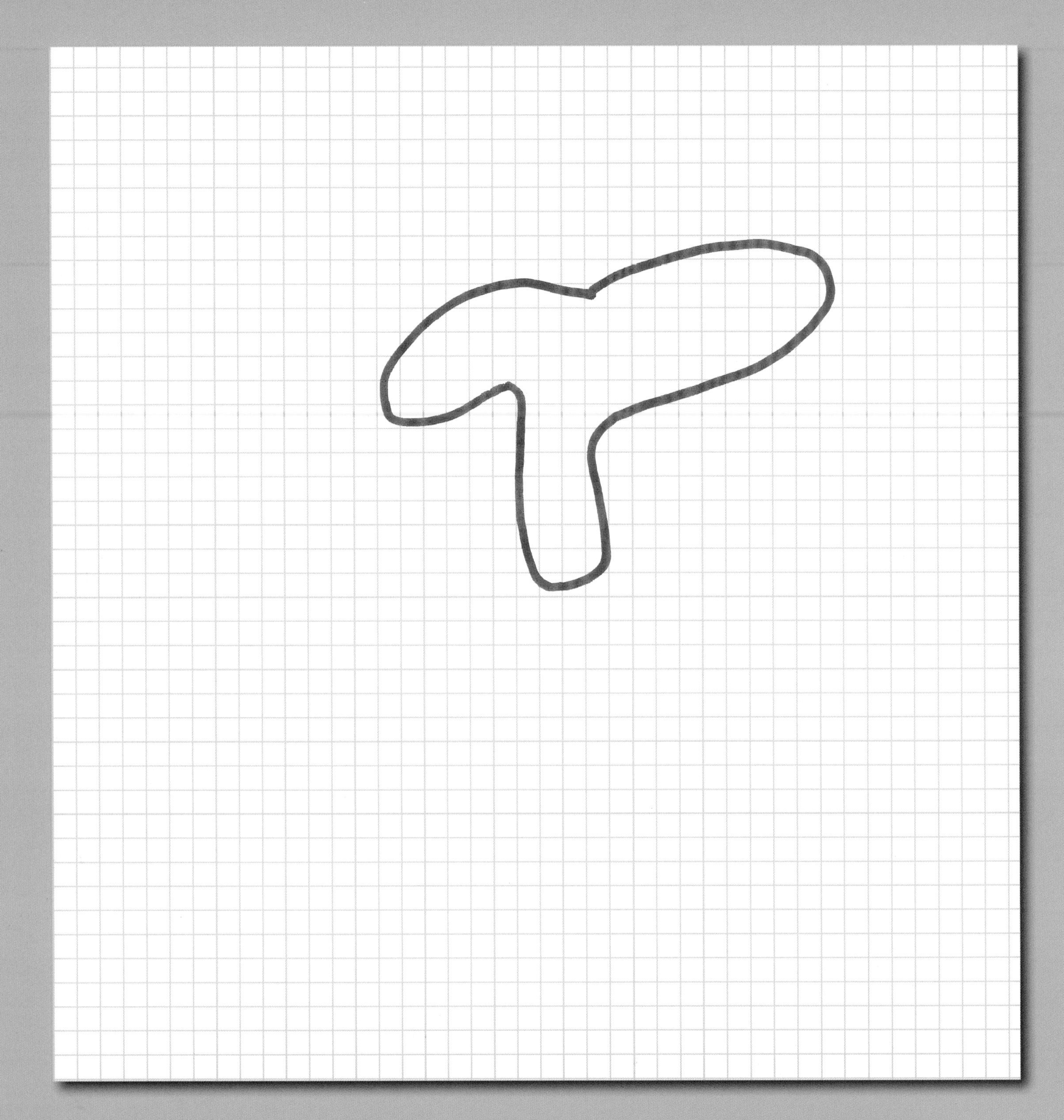

Bear looked at the shape ... and started to draw.

He turned the shape into a puppy.

"It's my turn now, Frida," said Bear.

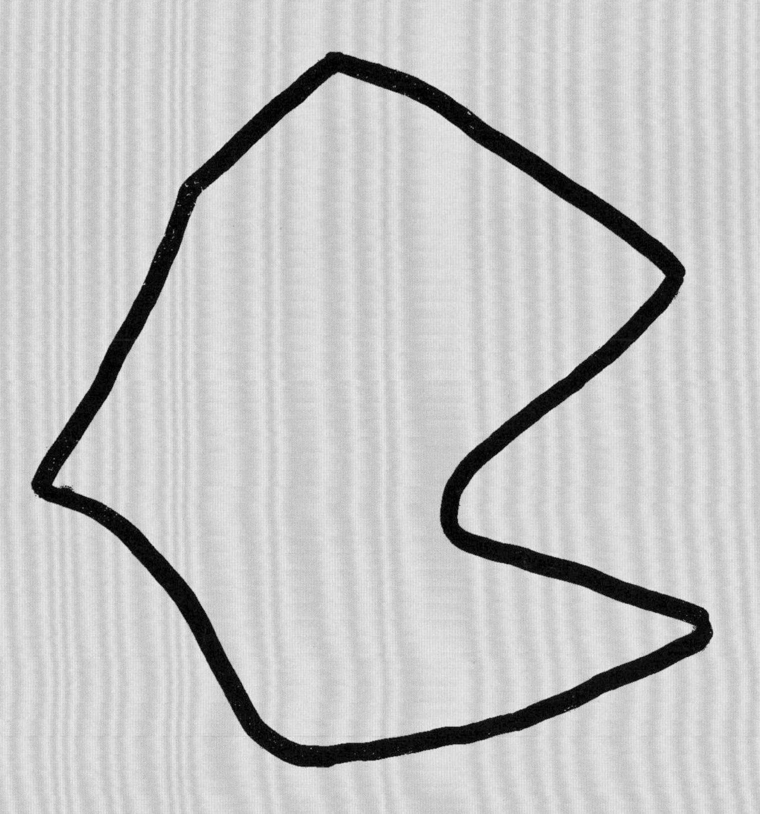

So he drew a shape, and passed it to Frida.

Frida turned it into a fish.

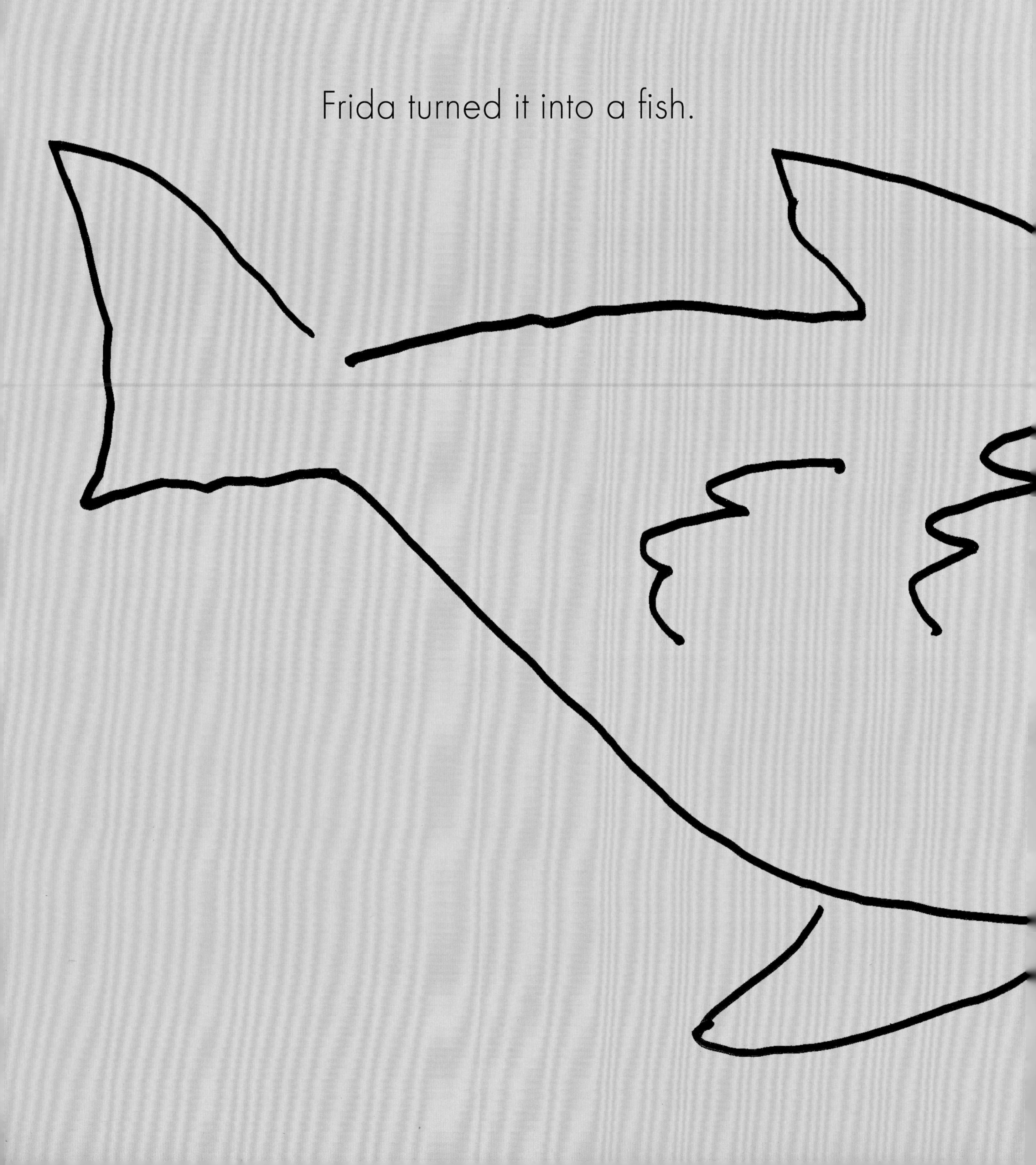

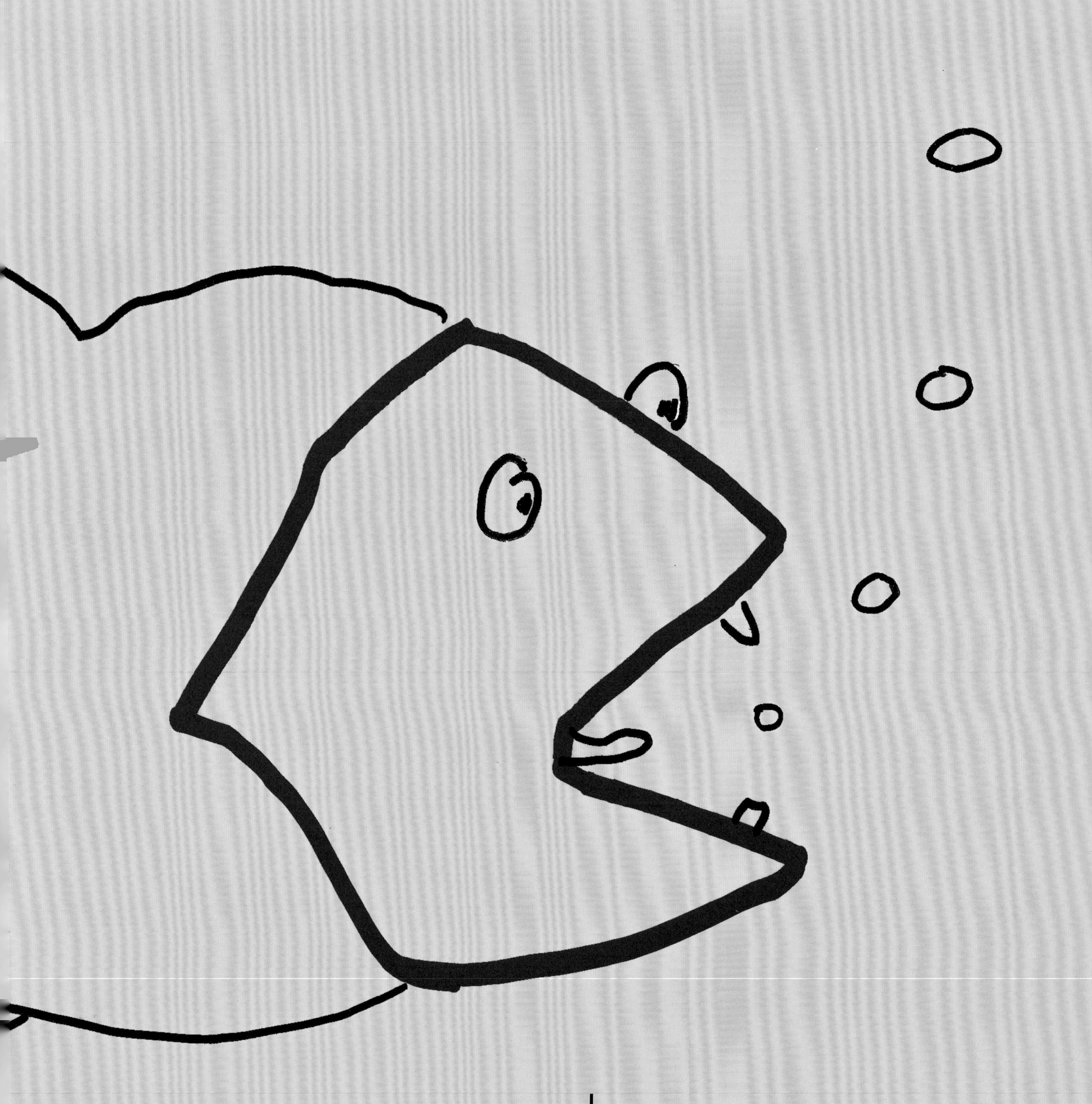

"Oooh, that's a big fish!" said Bear.

It was Frida's turn, so again
she drew a shape for Bear.

Bear thought for a while, then turned it into a pig.

"That's funny!" said Frida, laughing.

Bear made another shape...

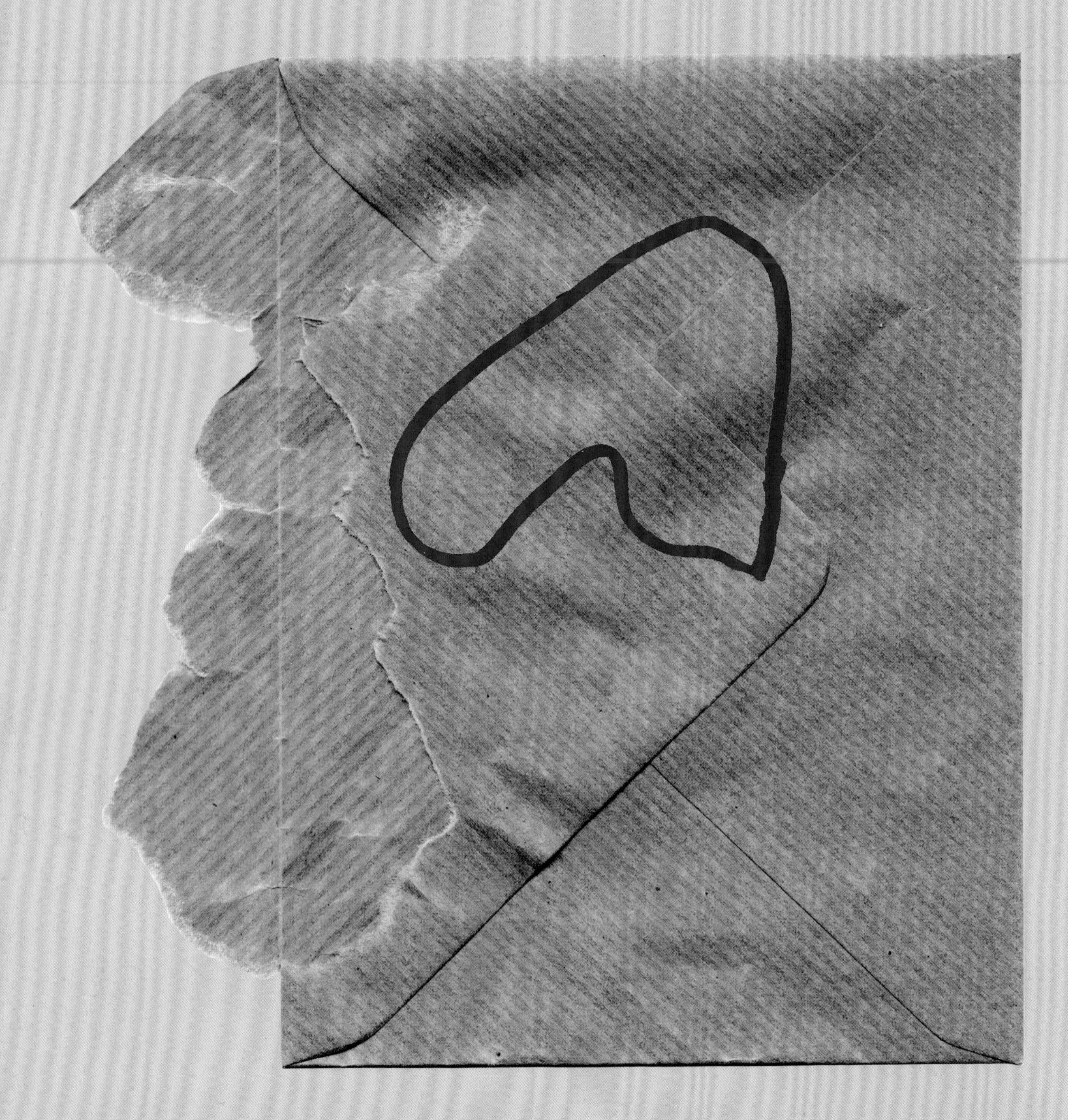

Frida turned it into a funny little man.

Frida gave Bear a piece of wrapping paper.

"I know what that looks like," said Bear,
and he began to draw.

"A monkey!" said Frida. "He looks cheeky."

Bear took a twig out of his pocket
and gave it to Frida.
"I wonder what that could be?" said Frida.
"Ah, I know!"

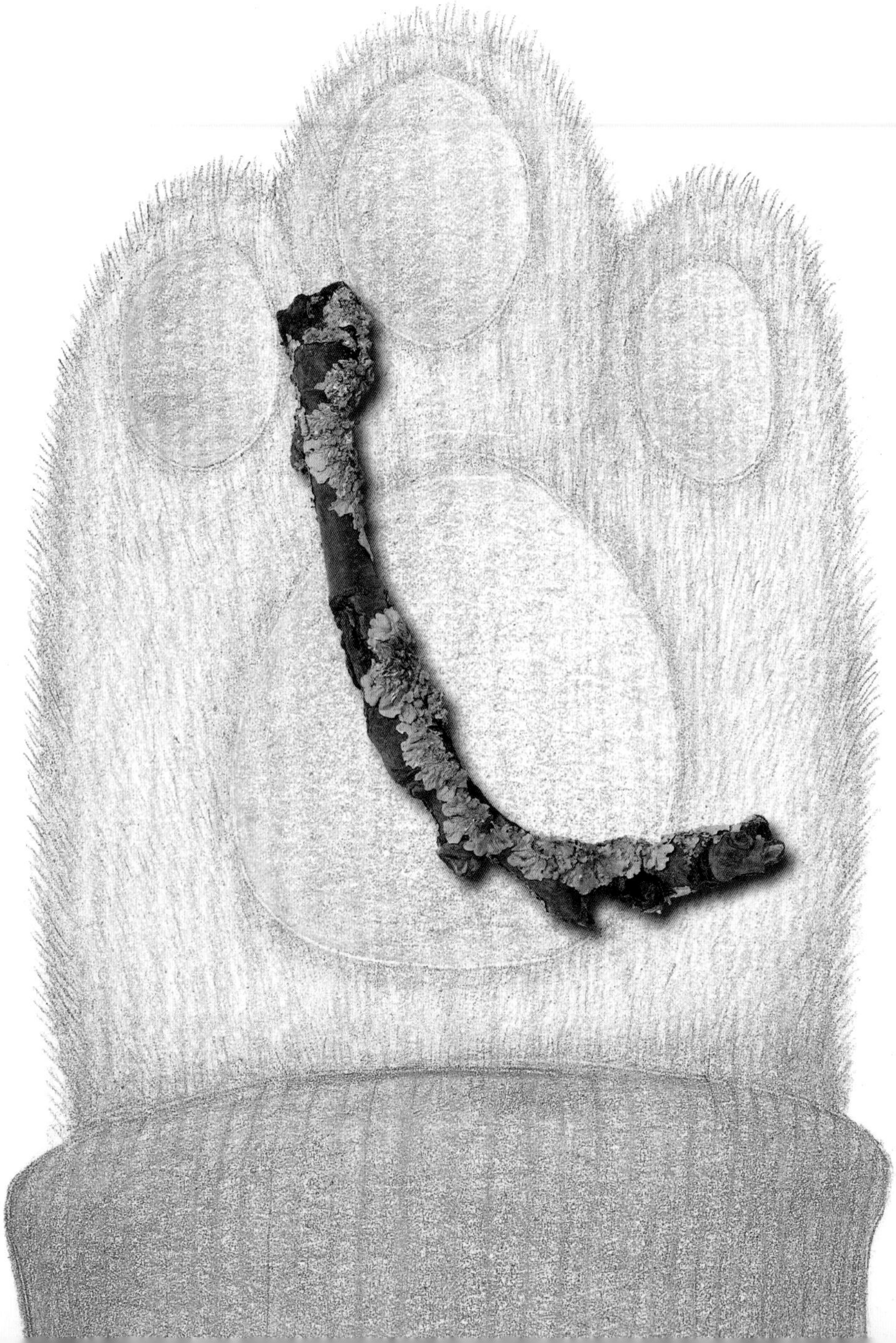

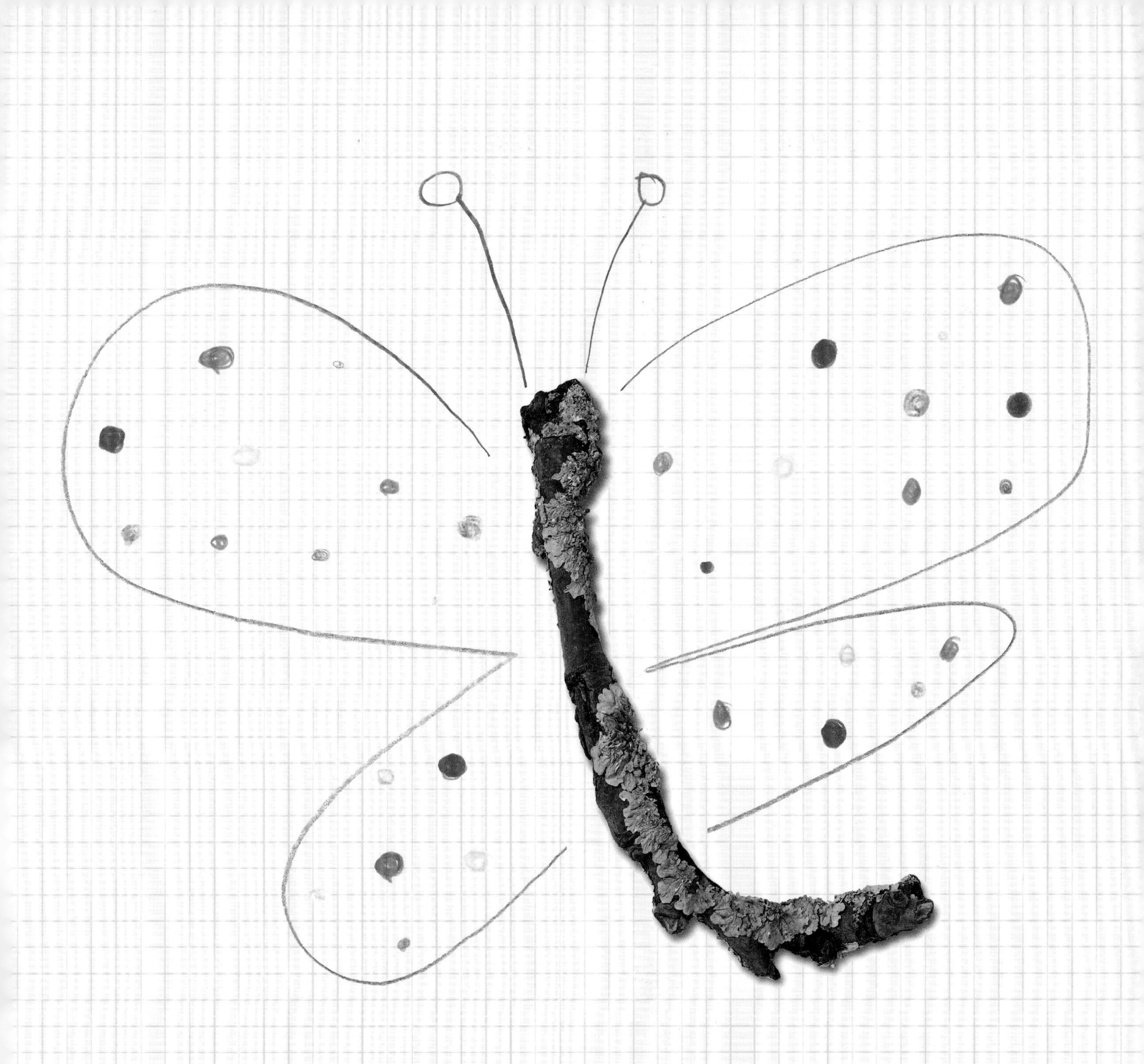

And Frida turned it into a butterfly.
"That's lovely!" said Bear. "Well done."

Frida and Bear love this game

and play it every day.

Look at all the pictures Frida and Bear have drawn!

Why don't you draw some
shapes and play?

Other books by Anthony Browne

Anthony Browne is one of the most celebrated author-illustrators of his generation. Acclaimed Children's Laureate from 2009 to 2011 and winner of multiple awards – including the prestigious Kate Greenaway Medal and the much coveted Hans Christian Andersen Award – Anthony is renowned for his unique style. His work is loved around the world.

ISBN 978-1-4063-1327-7

ISBN 978-1-84428-559-4

ISBN 978-1-4063-1328-4

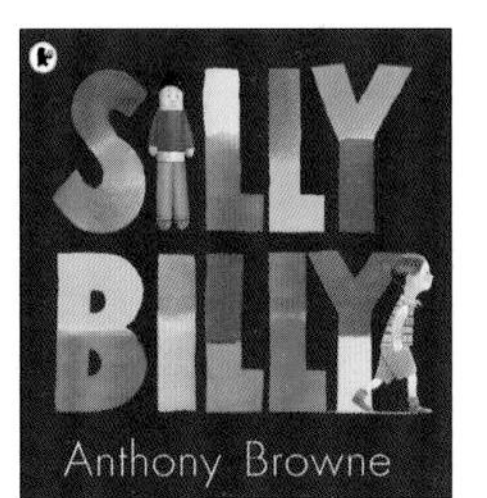

ISBN 978-1-4063-0576-0

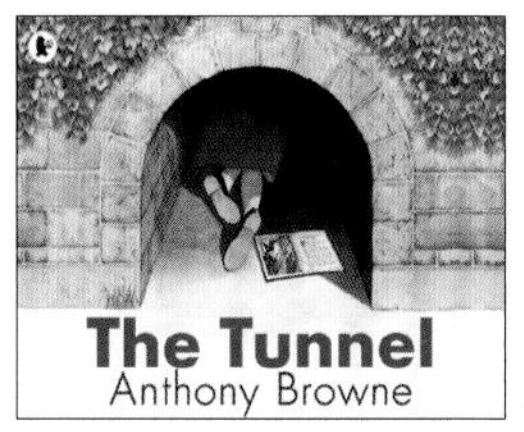

ISBN 978-1-4063-1329-1

ISBN 978-1-4063-1930-9
ISBN 978-1-4063-1852-4
ISBN 978-0-7445-9858-2
ISBN 978-1-4063-2187-6
Board book edition
ISBN 978-1-4063-3851-5
ISBN 978-1-4063-4791-3
Board book edition
ISBN 978-0-7445-9857-5
ISBN 978-1-4063-2178-4
Board book edition
ISBN 978-1-4063-2628-4
ISBN 978-1-4063-1874-6
ISBN 978-1-4063-1873-9
ISBN 978-1-4063-1356-7
ISBN 978-1-4063-1357-4
ISBN 978-1-4063-3131-8
ISBN 978-1-4063-1339-0
ISBN 978-1-4063-4162-1
ISBN 978-1-4063-4163-8
ISBN 978-1-4063-4164-5
ISBN 978-1-4063-4533-9

ISBN 978-1-4063-6089-9

Available from all good booksellers

www.walker.co.uk